Building
Net
Castles

Building
Net
Castles

Doughty tale of Digital Presence

Radhika Vijay

Dedicated to
"Lord Krishna"

For contact and more Information:
Radhika Vijay
https://www.ispharmacologydifficult.com
First Edition, 2022

Foreword

This book symbolises my entry in the genre of Fiction. I never realised this art of storytelling more precisely story writing within myself till I wrote this book.

It is up to you how you like it, I had great fun narrating these gripping dialogues and scenes from my self-woven yarn of imagination.

It is a light, fun story ending in a well to learn moral, as usual stories do. It is special in a way because of its proximity to contemporary setting, style and literature.

This story is for all, it is not bound to age and era.

With idiomatic twists and turns in the day to day dialogues and pictures of my imagined city and characters, I hope you enjoy reading this incidental piece of literature!

Don't forget to subscribe to my free E-Newsletter by simply signing up at https://www.ispharmacologydifficult.com . It contains a lot of updates about drugs, medicines, health and my podcast updates also. And now the *Author updates* section will be added to let you all know more!

Table Of Contents

Chapter 1: The Land of Otenz

Otenz, metropolitan city of skyscrapers and lakes garlanded by silver waters of the Reen and adorned by Glittery snowfall.

Reen almost splits the city in two parts. There are bridges across the river and boats sail by.

Faraway from the main city, across the river are found few small villages, while in the city the river banks are bedecked with Restaurants, one to name is the "Echo" restaurant and the Malls which form the heart and soul of the city. People hang here day and night and it's flooded during the weekends. Cafes are generally located near residential areas and Gyms are found in the Mall or the Supermarket.

Roads run all around the city , they are as clean as a whistle and as dark as coal-hole. They seem like studded with starry yellow and white taxis, cabs and cars, some colourful bikes look like firecrackers on the road, all truly within the eyeshot but out of this world!!

In the mainland are found both apartments and singular houses.

With plenty of cabs and taxis running by, the distances do not matter and people are found all around the city.

The river boats are not only wooden gewgaws but also utilitarian things. People economically and quickly move to and fro the river through these watercrafts.

Some young skilled folk choose staunch arch bridges instead which are too well

maintained and ornamented with a
variety of flowery and green ivy and
creepers.
Viewed from top, the city is fringed by
silver, golden, mirror and crystal like
skyscrapers.
The weather stays chilly and snowy with
occasional heat waves. This potpourri of
the climate makes the living of mankind
kaleidoscopic.
Shining like gems, chockablock with
elegance, through the lens of my pen,
deep reverence for Otenz!!

OTENZ

Chapter 2: Olivia's first day at Otenz

Olivia gets down the cab and asks for help from the driver to carry her luggage across the main iron gate of the house. Hearing the doorbell, Mrs Sanchez peeps through the doorhole and opens the door, she fails to recognise Olivia and asks her to introduce herself.

Olivia shows her Identity card and tells her that she is a student of Diet and Nutrition and has come to pursue higher studies at University of Otenz.

Mrs Sanchez quickly recalls the telephonic talk she had with Olivia a few days back. She calls her maid and asks her to help Olivia carry her luggage and proceeds to escort Olivia to her room. After climbing stairs for upto two floors, Olivia enters a dusky, dusty, grey walled room- a gloomy look as a first impression!

Room had a hall, in the centre of which there were two beds, one of them was made up tidily in accordance with a neat and clean wardrobe nearby, Olivia could easily recognise it as her own. While the other bed was messy with clothes and stationary stuff.

Olivia was extremely curious to find the attached kitchen place. Mrs Sanchez left her with the maid to arrange and organise her things and stuff.

The day passed by as a rough, rowdy, tired one. Grey walls of the room added to the despair, finally Olivia plunged into deep sleep.

The big bang of the door shook her up from the sleep and she rushed to open the door.

She was not expecting to meet a second stranger on the same day but to her surprise she had to go for it. The other young girl entered the room and threw her purse on the end of the other bed. She quickly picked her stuff like clothes and stationary from the bed and cleaned it all. She did not utter a word with Olivia that day and got busy with her own work. Olivia too was not keen in talking about her whereabouts and the day drifted quietly for both of them.

Chapter 3: Meeting Charlotte

Sun rose high on Sunday the next day. Surely there were no Cocks crowing in a city like Otenz to wake up and force people to abandon their reveries in vain. But the alarm hit hard enough for Olivia as she could not tolerate the noisy sound of it.

As she came to her senses, she saw the other girl sitting lazily on a chair nearby sipping her morning tea. Before Olivia could say anything, a voice murmured, "Good morning friend! Nice to see you, come join me for the tea now. Mrs Sanchez told me about your arrival though the date was not finalised. I was too tired yesterday and you seemed sleepy. I am Charlotte from a nearby town, staying here for my job in a Bank. What brings you here?"

Olivia introduced herself and narrated the cause of her stay in Otenz. Soon both cheered up and exchanged tete-a-tete delightfully over the Sunday morning tea.

Olivia felt like home after getting all her stuff organised and spending two more days with Charlotte. Both added vibrant hues to the grey walls of the room, it was all bright and pleasant!

Chapter 4: First day at University

It was time for real work now. Olivia had to kickstart her studies and attend the University from today!

It was high time to get engrossed in her course and curriculum and set about her new routine.

She was a student in a class of fifty. The class was divided into five groups of ten students each in alphabetical order.

On Friday, the last reading day of the week, all the students were in a hurry to set their weekend in motion. Class was too lengthy to bear today for all!

After the last discourse, Olivia was packing her bag, suddenly someone called her out loud, Olivia turned back and identified the person, she realised the freckled face she had seen in her group.

Hello! Hope you doin' well, I am Noah, in the same group by the way. I wanted to request a few days back notes, and I wanted to borrow them for the weekend, please."

Sure, I don't remember you were there a few days back, but certainly I saw you on Day 1 and then today, Right?"

"Yes, Actually, I am new to Otenz, and I travel every weekend to my place of residence , a village on Reen. Here I work as a consultant in one of the private Gyms. I have to earn for my family, hope you understand (smiles). Apart from college, life has many twists and turns too!"

"Yups! No problem, you can borrow, see ya on Monday, Bye!"

"Wait, please keep my professional card and if possible share it too, it's gonna help me."

Oh! Ok Thanks!

Noah rushed straight out while Olivia hired a cab to return to her room.

Charlotte was waiting for Olivia like anything to reveal her Vibgyor Weekend plans, exciting things to do like breakfast at Cafe Coffee Day, Sunday matinee followed by a shift from al desko to al fresco slap up meal.

As always, Olivia couldn't have better plans than these for exploring her first weekend in Otenz, she was all set to execute these fabulous schemes.

But before that she had tons and tons of conversations to convey and she showed Charlotte Noah's business card too!

Charlotte took a keen glance over it and made a nice remark about his social media platforms and webpage. She even hinted Olivia to add him on her Social media for quick nutrition tips.

Olivia was amazed at this advice as she was quite indecisive and ignorant about use of Social media. She was the kind of person who would lastly post anything on Social media, like a frog caught in well. She had her own notions and perceptions and was quite against use of Social media. Maybe the negative lot of information and news had struck her ideas hard to turn her against the use of Social media, a kind of taboo or more probably a waste of time and brain power.

"Social media is a waste!"

"No its not, you need to learn it before you comment on it"

"Yeah?"

"Oh yes, you see, every coin has heads and tails, Right?"

"But I have always heard and read about people falling into horrible traps, earning bad names, getting blocked, etc. That's why I criticise this surfing behaviour."

"That's ok! Media is highly criticised, but you can get familiar with it, why misuse or overuse it? You need to learn decent etiquette and enjoy the Magical world of social media and the internet from a distance. You can always give it a try, see Noah, the village guy simply surfing to earn money and gains from it."

"I think we need to postpone this wasteful contretemps and switch over to dinner and a Good night sleep! I am really looking forward to a great weekend now."

"As you wish(smiles)"

Weekend vibes took their turns and both gals spent a commendable time exploring and window shopping at a Supermall near their place, brunching at Cafe Coffee Day followed next day by Sunday matinee and a delightful dinner. Two days ended in highly tiresome but memorable times- a seventh cloud feeling!

Chapter 5: Firm Determination

On Monday, Noah returned the notebooks. Olivia made new friends, all exchanging comments and their social media handles. It was high time for Olivia to get interested in what all that seemed superfluous.

It took almost a week for her to finally decide to get herself showing up on Social media and Web.

She herself secretly inquired and searched for a Web solution company that could help her out to give her decisions a real form and shape. Yes she too wanted to get her webpage made! She quickly got ready on Saturday morning and after having routine breakfast, she hired a cab to the nearby supermall where the Web solution company office was located.

She climbed the stairs on the first floor hurriedly and knocked on the door.

She waited at the reception for almost an hour , when finally she was called to meet the Company chairman who headed all the proceedings and chores.

As Olivia entered the room, it was a spacious room with a centre table and chair and surrounding almirahs to keep and store documents.

The Chairman greeted and seated her in front of him and asked her to wait for 5 for minutes till he completed an urgent phone call.

Olivia looked around and was thinking of conveying her demands in accurate short sentences.

"Hello Miss, I am Dayne, nice to see you here, tell me about your idea and wish."

"Goodmorning Sir, I am Olivia, a student of Diet and Nutrition, I wanted your help to build a Web Page of mine and create basic social media handles, since this is not my cup of tea."

"Sure, That's our job, I need some basic information about your idea of webpage, its style, name and design, etc. and I will show you two or three created options, so that you can finalise one of them and start your online work."

"Oh, great, that is exactly my point of view and what I expected, thank you so much Mr Dayne. What are your charges for all this work, do let me know please."

"Well, all in all it is a never ending process, since once you start your work, I will initially charge you 2000 bucks and for the maintenance fee, you have to submit me 1000 bucks per month, is that fine?"

"Hmm, ok, yes, maybe, yes, it's fine, can you show me some of your accomplished endeavours? Can I get a little deduction in fees, actually you know, I am just a student, right?"

"We offer high quality services, Ms Olivia, so there is no question of fee deduction. My receptionist will show you some of our well accomplished online projects and you will be satisfied."

"Oh, ok, thank you." Olivia got up and returned back to the reception, all in a big confusion regarding fee payment. The receptionist showed her all the wonderful achievements of the company in no time. She asked Olivia to deposit half of the initial amount so that her dream project is commenced without any delay. Still confused but determined, she deposited 1000 bucks and the receptionist asked her to find a good project name, design idea, profile pic, etc for her online webpage and social media handles. Olivia's face lit up with glee!

She was on seventh cloud and couldn't resist herself to narrate the day's events to her roommate.

"Hey ! Charlotte! Do you have any idea where I have been all day?"

"Nopes."

"You know, today was my day of moving forward towards making my social media accounts."

"Really? You are seriously getting into this? Are you?"

"Yups! And I did work for it today. I visited a Web Solution office and paid them to get my things started."

"Hmm! Are you sure they have a good reputation in their field ? You see, I don't want you to be swindled, hope you understand."

"Yes, they do! The receptionist showed me many projects of their achievement and customer satisfaction. I did trust them and paid 1000 bucks."

"Are you nuts! You should have at least waited for your work to be finished. Now there's no point in regretting , hope all turns out well and planned."

"It will be fine, I am sure, let us pin today's moments with some chocolate scoops I have got for both of us(giggles)"
"Oh my God, you nailed it, thank you so much, may you achieve success in your efforts"
Both the girls made merry before they wished each other Good night!

Chapter 6: Rising high with Hard work

Dreams were getting bigger, the University lectures classes were shrinking small. Olivia was bewitched by the Virtual luminosity. She couldn't help thinking about her digital presence. It was nothing unusual yet a diamond in Olivia's pocket.

In a two day span, she was sitting at Web Solutions with her self created website design, name, logo and a pic for her different social media handles.

Mr Dayne took all the documents and details and assured her to finish all her work as per her desires and demands in a fortnight duration. Too long for Olivia, yet worthwhile, so she was happy about it.

Fortnight passed in a coon's age for Olivia, though she finished her class work and home chores patiently and managed to keep a poker's face.

The big day arrived and Olivia hived herself off the class discourse though physically was present there. She reached the Web Solutions office at two o'clock in the afternoon.

Her patience was tried for another hour and finally she was called to meet Mr Dayne. She entered his room like a student ready to receive his results after an exam.

With an insouciant shrug, Mr Dayne picked up his phone and called the receptionist.

As soon as she arrived, Mr Dayne asked the receptionist to show Olivia her webpage. The receptionist escorted

Olivia out of the room and showed her webpage.

It was a Red letter day for Olivia. She took the sharing link from the receptionist and went back to her room.

Charlotte did not arrive by evening 6 pm and this was Olivia's second forbearance examination in the same day.

As the clock struck 7:30 pm, Charlotte arrived and Olivia let the cat out of the bag.

It was a shining time for both of them and they decided to dine out that day as a token of jollification.

Olivia shared the link from the receptionist at all her social media handles and was expecting a handful of followers or clients in a few days.

She actually had a stupendous response from around more than 500 people including her classmates.

Within a period of 3 months, she had a good gracious following and had started building up a loyal clientele. Now she was suggested by many of her clients to alter a few sections of her webpage, change some design and make a proper work website for herself.

It was time for another visit to the Web Solutions Office.

Chapter 7: Getting tricked

It was Friday noon time and the hot spell broke, Olivia rushed upwards the staircase and quickly entered the Web Solution reception area. She requested the receptionist to arrange a talk with Mr Dayne.

It was quickly managed and Olivia asked if few changes in her Webpage could be done. Mr Dayne displayed utter forgetfulness and asked Olivia the name of her Webpage and different social media handles. Olivia gave him the details. Now when Mr Dayne glanced at her profile, it was much different from what he had made or expected.

Olivia's hard work had shown tangible results. Her huge following and web traffic nonplussed Mr Dayne. He was debased and out of spite he told Olivia that changes to the webpage are very difficult and require more manpower and technical skills. He agreed to do all the designing and website fabrication only if Olivia pays her 5000 bucks more to hire skilled manpower.

In a great dilemma, a situation of being in sticky wicket, Olivia impulsively paid him 5000 bucks.

She had lost her senses and when she reached her room she was tired and befuddled.

Somehow she felt humbugged. Struck by deep anguish and utter despair, she made an unpleasant tea for herself , went out on the terrace and sat on the patio.

Each sip was hitting hard, she finished the tea and went back to the room. She never got to know when she had an hour-long siesta and woke up with the knocking noise of the door.

When she opened the door, Mrs Sanchez was standing, smiling with a plate full of cake pieces in her hands.

"Hello Aunty! How are you? And these cake chunks? What happened?"

"It's Mr Sanchez' birthday today, why don't you join us both for dinner, we will be very glad if you do."

"Sure, that's my pleasure, I was waiting for Charlotte, it is ok, I'll wash my face and come down."

Chapter 8: Silver Lining

Mrs Sanchez lit the evening lamp as a custom of their Spiritual procedures and prayers. She had a beautifully decorated home temple. To make Mr Sanchez' birthday more of a memorable one, she had decorated the temple with fresh flowers and scents, all in all the whole house was scented with the fragrance of Camphor and Sandalwood. The dining space was in continuation with the kitchen. Three of them seated around the round dining table. The prepared food was placed in the centre of the table. While Mrs Sanchez served the hot vegetable curry, Mr Sanchez read Olivia's face and asked her, "Is everything Ok? You look a little lost, what happened?"

Olivia was not interested in dragging Mr
or Mrs Sanchez in her newly created
whole raft of problems, but at the same
time she could not pretend that black is
white and eventually spilled the beans
over the dinner table.

"Oh my God! 5000 bucks he charged,
right?" exclaimed Mrs Sanchez

"No, I have paid him about 7000 bucks
till now. I feel incarcerated, hope you
feel the same way for me?"

"Of course dear!" Mr Sanchez agreed
while he took his specs down to clean
them of some dust.

"Tell me Uncle! What can I do now?
How to save my webpage and get rid of
this mountebank? I just cannot tolerate
this cozener."

"I know, I have an idea, you ask him to transfer the domain rights to you, even if he asks for more money."

"You think it's gonna work?"

"Yes, Let us wait and watch. You do as I say. Hey, would you like to have a panoramic view of Reen banks? Me and Aunty were planning to go out after dinner, you join us, the Natural riverscape is breathtaking, do not stew, let's go."

Silver waters of Reen reflected as silver lining in Olivia's head and heart. After a stone's throw away stroll, three of them returned back. She kept Charlotte unaware of her plans and waited for the sunrise patiently.

Chapter 9: The Denial

Today was Saturday and Olivia was not sure if the office of Web Solutions was open or not. She chose a comfortable time and started ringing the receptionists' phone number. Luckily she picked up Olivia's phone.

"Hello mam, are you all open today?"

"Well, not officially, but yes, we all will be there for 2-3 hours, that's it and then we will wrap up."

"Ok, can I come for an urgent talk with Mr Dayne?"

"Let me ask him first, if he is free and has no appointments. I will message you the meeting time."

"Thank you so much mam."

Olivia's day drifted with hard luck, two hours passed by , then suddenly the receptionist called her to come.

Olivia reached the place in no time, before she could say anything, the receptionist asked her what she wanted.

"I need to talk to Mr Dayne , please connect me to him."

"I will try."

The receptionist hurried to Mr Dayne's room and returned back with a blank face.

"What Happened? Is he there?"

"Yes, he has only 20 minutes for you, you can go inside."

"Oh! Thanks."

"Hello Mr Dayne. I wanted to talk to you about something very important."

"Yeah! Tell me Ms Olivia."

"I was wondering, Mr Dayne, it would be a nice idea if I could have the ownership of my domain name , you see I hardly have time to visit your Office again and again. I have to study also. If I owe my domain, whatever little corrections or changes I feel like doing, I will try to handle them on my own. Right? What do you think?"

"Hmm, that is a smart idea Ms Olivia, but I need to let you know that domain names are not dime store stuff that you can afford whenever you want. It will be a ritzy deal, that will really irk you, better let go of this gormless proposal. You won't find better Web designers than us all around Otenz."

Mr Dayne's hubristic words ruffled Olivia's feathers. She kept still and calm.

"I will think about it Mr Dayne and let you know later, thanks for your valuable time."

"Your wish Miss", Mr Dayne uttered
with an evil grin.

The sky fell on Olivia, a rewind muddle
of all her losses, Mr Dayne's words and
behaviour were breaking her desires and
dreams. She still couldn't believe it!

Chapter 10: Piece of Advice

Olivia entered the iron gate around half past 4 in the evening, and she realised that Mrs Sanchez was eagerly looking for her return. She called Olivia directly in her house. They all sat in the dining space and Mr Sanchez too arrived.

"So, how was your day, my dear girl? Did you go to the web designing Office? Did they hear you?"

"Yes, Uncle, I did go and have just returned from there only. Mr Dayne was least interested in my proposal and he actually indirectly refused (sadly). I was astounded by his cavalier and deriding words and expressions, Whatever! I am still puzzled and thinking of a way out of these abrupt and unforeseen banana skins."

"Oh! Please don't worry, this sitch may be a curate's egg, who knows?" Mrs Sanchez comforted Olivia.

"See dear, Don't jump into conclusions, It is not the end of the world, I mean this world on the internet (laughs). I know it may sound a little bitter, but let bygones be bygones, don't chase the unreachable realities, it would be wise enough to get started again on your own. If I had known before I would have never allowed you to pay in excess to that Web company, you could have saved the losses. It's the right time to turn these stumbling blocks into stepping stones to success."

"Thank you Uncle for showing me the way out of this dilemma, I will surely pay heed to your piece of advice, it is

dark now, I need to talk to Charlotte too.
Good night to both of you!”
“Charlotte! Open the door, it is me
Olivia!”
“Where have you been?Is everything
fine?” Olivia narrated all events and
Charlotte too agreed with Uncles’ piece
of advice.

Chapter 11: New Beginning

Sunday was new and real, Olivia had wiped the slate clean and as it was all a fresh start for her. She enrolled in some free courses about basics of Website making and Social media handles and read books on the same topic from the city library.

Over a fortnight duration, she was able to figure out her new dream online project and get over the doomed scenario.

She put her nose to the grindstone and with some new and many old followers, again enjoyed the company of a loyal clientele.

She was fully determined to never conjure up and keep on working quietly and consistently towards her goal.

It was second year in the University and after the setback, Olivia had grown up to be much consolidated and consistent towards her goals. She had actually learnt many basic skills to work efficiently online all on her own and without spending a single penny.

Her good social media contacts brought her good favours and many times unexpected gifts and earnings. All her hard work and perseverance was rewarded in a glittery manner.

One day one of her long-time followers returned from a foreign place and requested to visit her on the way back. Olivia was overwhelmed to meet this lady client for the first time as she showed her gratitude by offering floral decoratives and chocolate cupcakes. Her kind gesture filled Olivia's heart with gratitude and served as a catalyst to work patiently and consistently and never give up. Endurance and Guts can help float high the rough waves of adversity.

These were the learnings of Olivia in a course of a year after the unwelcome course of events she had been through. Her studies took on a smooth course and she was aiming for a sound career opportunity after passing out of University.

Chapter 12: The Lucky Birthday

One of the evenings, Olivia was strolling amidst the cool breezy weather on the terrace outside her room, when suddenly the phone rang. Olivia did not recognise the phone number and thought of it to be of a new client, based on her day to day experience. She picked up the phone call, and to her surprise, a familiar sound came.

"Hello, is this Miss Olivia?"

"Yes, I am speaking, tell me, who is there?"

"Miss Olivia, I am speaking from Web Solutions, we have not received your monthly fee for the last six months or more. If you do not pay the pending fee in 5 days, your webpage and related links and accounts will be terminated forever."

"Oh! Ok, I will see and call you back soon"

"Ok Miss Olivia, have a good day!" Charlotte arrives meanwhile and asks Olivia about how her day went by. Olivia tells Charlotte about the Phone call.

"Oh God! They called you again? That owner of the company is highly covetous, he is still longing for some monetary gains out of you?What does he think? All fools rush into his office."

"That is fine, I will not reply to them, rather block their phone number. Let them do whatever they want. I am determined not to pay heed to these trivial affairs any more. By the way, today is my birthday, let us move out and celebrate."

"Great! I think we should ask Mr and Mrs Sanchez too to go along with us." Quickly both the girls run down the stairs to ask for the landlords' company.

Knock! Knock!

"Hello Uncle and Aunt, It is Olivia's birthday today. We would like to invite you both to an early dinner in "Echo" restaurant on the banks of river Reen."

"Oh! That's wonderful! Happy birthday dear Olivia!" exclaimed Mrs Sanchez. Mr Sanchez too gave blessings to Olivia on this wonderful day.

All four of them hired a cab and reached "Echo" restaurant in about an hour. They got seated in the outer balcony covered with greenery and shed. The beautiful silver waters of Reen could be seen glittering with added hues of golden sunset.

"So, tell me Olivia, how's your online endeavours going on? Hope all is smooth and fine now."

"Yes, Uncle, my virtual whereabouts are all running smooth and fine now. Once I pass my exams, I will try to set up my consultation locus too. That's simply a flash of an idea, I am not worried about it at present though."

"That is a great idea, Ohk tell me the name of your webpage, I will too visit it virtually"

"Sure, It is named as Olivia's Nutrihub"

"Nice name. Let me find it, Ok I found it. It is there on the first page of search results and I see a small box on the upper right hand corner with your name, ``What's that?"

Charlotte too has a glance on Uncle's phone and exclaims, "Oh! This is a knowledge panel! Hey, Olivia, did you see your panel? You are lucky to get one, Today's celebration is increasing manifolds! Hurray!"

"Really? It must have just started showing on search results. I never noticed before. Oh wow! It is a great feeling. Thanks to God! Thanks to all of you for always being at my side to encourage and prop up my efforts. A big cheer to all of us! Yeah! (loudly)"

Poem

BUILDING NET CASTLES

I will narrate

A doughty tale

In Otenz' landscape

By the Reen's

silver Adam's ale

Olivia had a vision

A great determination

Was a friendly lass

Charlotte's bosom pal

Incandescent Noah's notion

Guided Olivia's course of action

Countless visits

To Mr Dayne's office

Went in vain

Diminution of gains

Mrs Sanchez' words of kindness

Brought some alleviation
Mr Sanchez' fantastic pointers
Illuminated the inky and gloomy
junctures
Painstaking and persistent trials
Fetched Olivia her panel
Reverie of every mind's marbles
To build their own net castles!
                    -Dr Radhika Vijay

Meet the Characters

Olivia

Charlotte

Mr & Mrs
Sanchez

Noah

Mr Dayne

Receptionist

Afterword

Thanks for reading and making up this far!
Hope the book served your expectations and
curiosity!

And you can also subscribe on different social
media like Twitter, Instagram, Facebook and
Youtube.
And once again, don't forget to subscribe for
my E-Newsletter on
www.ispharmacologydifficult.com

Acknowledgements

I especially want to mention a vote of thanks to my family, especially my son who is always interested in my books and this serves as a catalyst to my writing ventures!!
Next a great thanks to Mom and my brother for always being there by my side through thick and thin!
And never to forget , heartiest thanks to the readers, "You are the best!"

About The Author

Dr Radhika Vijay , MBBS, MD Pharmacology belongs to Bikaner, Rajasthan, India. She is a faculty in Sardar Patel Medical College, Bikaner.

She has always been an elite student since her school days. She has been teaching Medical Pharmacology for the last 10 years now and with this book she has ventured her skills in genre Fiction too!!

Appreciator of everything brilliant and intelligent in life and. with an optimistic attitude and approach she believes in the value and power of time, prayers and purpose driven consistency as strong foundation elements in one's life!

You can connect:

Personal Website - https://www.drradhikavijay.com

Podcast Website:

https://www.ispharmacologydifficult.com

Twitter : https://twitter.com/IsPharmacology

Facebook:

https://www.facebook.com/ispharmacology.difficult.5

Instagram:

https://www.instagram.com/ispharmacologydifficult/

Youtube:

https://www.youtube.com/channel/UC-LnUrZKlcBuQaLa2HDQOVg